FEATHER ROUSING

FEATHER ROUSING

a hybridiary

REBECCA MEACHAM

BLACK LAWRENCE PRESS

Black Lawrence Press

Executive Editor: Diane Goettel
Chapbook Editor: Lisa Fay Coutley
Cover Art: "Yearnings" by Heather Schroeder
Book Cover and Interior Design: Zoe Norvell

Copyright © Rebecca Meacham 2024

ISBN: 978-1-62557-843-3

Excerpt(s) from *The Color Master*: Stories by
Aimee Bender, copyright © 2013 by Aimee Bender. Used by permission
of Doubleday, an imprint of the Knopf Doubleday Publishing Group,
a division of Penguin Random House LLC. All rights reserved.

Published 2024 by Black Lawrence Press.
Printed in the United States.

And the darkness, eating light, and again light,
and again light, lifted.

—Aimee Bender, "The Devourings"

TABLE OF CONTENTS

Feather Rousing

I.

In 1859, Charles Valentin Alkan writes a funeral march for a parrot. *This piece is a reconciliation*, he notes. *Forgive he who commemorates a defunct parrot!*

He begs apology as singers wail, in French, *Polly, Want a Cracker?* He is famously obsessive. If he plays a piece poorly, he plays it again, despite the yawning of the crowds, the yearning of their bladders.

His letters are embroidered with regret, his character serially self-stabbed, a tortured needlepoint. He waits behind doors for empty halls. He tests maids with hidden clutter. He even frets the butter. His house is two separate apartments, stacked atop each other. When guests call downstairs and he's above, the concierge states truthfully that nobody is home.

Years ago, he and Chopin swirled among the frilled. Everyone split their sides laughing, Chopin wrote. But in 1859, Chopin's dead and Alkan wears black on days he ventures out. He is mistaken for a cleric.

So what are we to do with his new song, this lark, this elegy yoking bird to bassoon?

II.

My husband says a song is a song, and not a person.

I say a song is a song *and* a person.

Songs are songs, he says.

My husband teaches himself guitar. His side gig was once spinning records.

But I played piano as a kid, so I know a song can be a battle so fierce it drove my father to part his corporate executive's hair into braids, just to mimic mine. My father bet me he could learn my recital piece in a day. He practiced his hands to blisters. My mom judged our contest. I won.

I know singing solo on stage opened a cello in my chest, forever swallowing my squeak of shyness.

I know "Hamilton" beats like my mother's great heart and looks like my daughters in summer nightgowns, twirling on cooling asphalt.

I know the alto parts of masses. I know the ingenue's "I want" songs. I know that a certain Christmas carol is the last song our high school's goalie sang before he shot himself in the head. I know that duets can power drives from Keystone to Key West. For years, I could not tell where my voice ended and someone else's began.

Once, I learned about super-flocks: clouds of birds a mile long that pivot, soar, and drop. They move in harmony. At that time, I hadn't been in a choir for twenty years.

I wept with loneliness.

That's what a song is, I tell my husband, a poet. But I fumble the metaphor. Besides, doesn't everyone and their mother compare music to birds?

III.

Alkan, too, left listeners dumbstruck. One wrote, "I couldn't begin to describe where the melody, penetrating the mystery of Death itself, climbs up to a blaze of light."

But when Alkan went into seclusion, tongues began to wag. *He sired a secret son*, they twittered. *The married mother was his student!*

Alkan tutored his son until the young man could tour theaters. Perhaps one afternoon in 1859, hands together on the keys, father and son noodled through notions of feathered funerals. Perhaps they pursed their lips in prim pretense.

Perhaps this is why, eleven years later, as Germans invaded, Alkan's son fled Paris with 121 cockatoos.

IV.

The notes of Alkan's "Trio in G Minor" flutter like birds fluffing their feathers, *feather rousing* the falconers call it, like the cardinal couple in our garden, tending to their nest: the flame-red father and muted mother swoop and hop through grass—Wisconsin in June is the greenest green there is, lush where days before, kids sledded their front yards. My family matches eggshells to *Can you see the babies?* We Google and gasp, because no matter the splendor of their fathers, baby birds look hideous, like something Mother Nature sneezed.

In a day, our hatchlings' heads poke up; next, they've perched.

This is why I'm now inspecting what seems like an empty nest.

It is not.

A fledgling screams and springs and falls feebly to earth.

And runs.

Don't fear me, come near me, here! I call.

The rumpled fledgling stares.

Of course, as a human, I know best. I twice return it to the nest. It twice defies my earnestness. It stumbles over open lawns towards steady parent songs.

Forgive me, fledgling, I say, exiling myself from your world. I regret causing your funeral.

V.

Sometimes our rescues come with wings: once, my husband carried an injured owl from road to rehab center; once we trapped a bat in a cup and freed it into midnight. Will our young cardinal thrive or die? I tell the story as a joke, yet I sew regret to hope with a thousand beaking stabs.

Sometimes our rescues are songs: Court and spark. Heart and soul. Thriller. You are the sunshine of my life.

Today, my husband texts, *The young cardinals are alive and well, red and gray and flying.*

All of Alkan's music is, some say, reconciliation.

So:

A song is, and is not, a person.

A song is also a bird.

Wait, wait, I'll make it better:

A song is a fledgling caged in your hands, bone and feather, skin and talon, unnested, unwieldy, like a note sent between people in love, like guideposts in our blindspots, bridging presence and absence, grief and hilarity, a tiny immensity—poised for release, ready to rouse.

Dreamland

Coney Island, 1904

Small enough to fit in the palm of your hand, Ladies and Gentlemen!
Peas in pods! Living dolls!
The stork was early but we're open late!
Don't pass the babies by!

The babies know nothing of their advertising, of course. All they know of life is heat. They've already forgotten their mothers' skin. They've never grabbed their fathers' thumbs, never suckled breast or bottle. The babies have no idea what they're missing. How could they? They have neither wish nor reflex; they haven't grown appetites. The babies sleep in the Bavarian farmhouse on the midway with its watchful plaster stork, lined up in gleaming incubators, defying all expectation. They are *frail cherubs*; they are *mites of humanity*. They are 10 cents a ticket.

Their births: a sudden soak of surprise. Their mothers' ankles puddled with dread, boots washed in unspent weight. The mothers tried to keep them home. They fretted the failed fashioning of wombs: stove-side boxes, hot-water bottles, flannel, hay. They worried the babies' weary eyes and oddly wrinkled foreheads. They are less newborns than dying old men, thought one, a mother of triplets. Now, she kisses their raw, red skin and lets the babies go. Their father, like all the babies' fathers, marvels at how light and spindly they are to lift, like birds' nests—like something, perhaps, blown away before the hatch of open mouths.

So go the babies, box to box. Down the fairway full of foods the father can't afford, past the breezy bridge where skirts fly high and couples clutch, locked-legged, breast to chest. The father finds the Bavarian farmhouse, a plaster stork perched on the roof. He hands the box to a white-capped nurse; Nurse lifts the lid and summons Doctor. Together—a man, a woman, three babies between them, and none of them in love—they disappear into the back. The father taps his taskless toes. Before him, boxed in glass, are babies, seven in a row. Crowds press forward—somehow the father hadn't noticed forty people warming the air with whispers. Then Nurse wheels three new glass boxes into place. People cheer. Name cards are affixed: Clara, Cora, Cate.

The father makes it to Midget City before he takes a breath. Tiny men drive tiny fire engines to put out tiny fires. The father waits to feel unburdened. Nothing is as he expects. What is he doing on this bench, watching the world move in garish miniature?

Down the fairway, babies sleep. They sleep as Nurse tips a narrow spoon of breast milk—defatted, calibrated—into their nostrils. They sleep as black-veiled women watch and dab their cheeks with lace. They sleep as men crunch peanuts and boys bump girls and old ladies gossip: which one has grown the most? Each day at noon, Nurse removes her giant diamond ring, lifts a baby's arm and slides it on his wrist: *That's right, Ladies and Gentlemen, a diamond ring around his wrist!*

The babies make no protest. Even with their eyelids open, they look asleep, suspended in the state of making, focused on becoming.

Soon, a woman passes through. Her hat is red—chosen for its clarity. She is too shy to part the crowd. She saves her pennies for returns. She's trying to learn what everyone knows is simple human instinct. Sometimes when Nurse lifts a baby to face the crowd, the woman in the red hat feels a stirring—it might be called concern. But what does she know of motherhood? A silly hat? A weekly visit? This row of bright machines?

The woman in the red hat returns in daylight. She returns in sleep. She dreams the babies fat and smooth; she dreams them roly-poly. She dreams one baby takes Nurse's diamond ring and cuts a perfect circle. Pop! The baby breaks the glass. She hears the babies crying, laughing, babbling their first words.

Go home, they're saying. Go home.

Are the babies scolding? Blaming? Pleading? What is she to do? Thousands interpret their cries each day; she should have learned by now. But the fairway is deserted, no one watching but the plaster stork. She can walk away, leave forever. Or she can step right up.

The babies have passed from nurse to nurse. They've spent their lives as numbers: science in a box. The woman in the red hat just wants to see the faces of her daughters. *Hers.* Her Clara, Cora, Cate.

Her daughters cry: Go home? It's the hardest, simplest thing to answer. But just like that, she gathers them—a wondrous weight that shifts her endless wait to ballast. No one parts a curtain, calling, *Touch their dimples! Hold them close and kiss their heads!* The space within her arms is theirs: quiet, beyond measure. Something rises in their hearts. Something is taking wing.

Plumage

Green Bay, 2020

From the edge of our backyard woods, turkeys stroll the greening grass, dripping April rain.

When my husband and I brought our second daughter home, we couldn't picture another baby in the house. *Two kids under two?* we worried. *How do people do it?* Then we pulled into our driveway where a turkey couple strolled with nineteen fuzzy fledglings.

Nineteen! we counted. And we kept counting as spring turned into summer, then fall, nineteen that stayed together as cars sped by and owls hooted from predatory perches, nineteen as my husband and I fumbled the double stroller, chasing after a toddler while soothing the world's hungriest newborn.

Then, hope was literally a thing with feathers—nineteen things, in fact. Outside, hope took ungainly wing and gobble-gobbled from the trees. Inside, hope kicked its fat baby legs in a Baby Björn strapped to my husband's chest and hope stomped the floors in our toddler's light-up sneakers. Hope threaded through our matching campaign shirts as we watched Obama's first inauguration.

Oh, the audacity of that hope.

They've grown—those birds, our birds—and now the world we've made for them seethes with viral fevers. On Facebook Live, old white men warn of droplets and old white men deny droplets and old white men wear masks and old white men mock masks.

Our daughters nest all day in bed, clicking through moved-online schoolwork and snapchatting their squads, their own loud flocks now out-of-sync and scattered over zip codes. Their teachers try their best. I get it. I've moved my writing workshops from seminar table to desktop iMac, where I tune in, live, wearing the increasingly weird T-shirts I order late at night, where our once rambling, funny class discussions are bingo-carded into "raise hand," "join," and "mute." My husband, a college Dean, powers through problems of kilns and chorales as students violate apartment noise limits to practice oboe and students sit in hometown parking lots to take exams on iPhones. My mother, at 80, loathes the thought of her fragility, so we add vocabulary to the language of our eternal compromise: senior hours, curbside pick-up, double-layer masking, sanitize, aerosolize, spread.

And yet, our house is a gilded cage that I secretly adore. We're all here, together, my family, in love, in health, alive. It's unspeakable—it's a kind of gluttony, I know—to feel contentment in amidst so much grief and misery.

But listen: from her bedroom, our teenager plucks her ukulele and sings about boys she may or may not decide, someday, to love. Her voice is strong and bright and constant.

And look: where there once wailed a newborn, a tween waits for our daily drive-thru coffee run. She's put on lipstick. She wears a new Hawaiian shirt. She will not set foot in a public space for another year.

Outside, the turkeys huddle together and shake off the rain.

Inside, our hope sheds and grows like plumage.

The Lady, The Tiger
Cincinnati, 1999

Home now, beside you, your tiger sleeps. He has been sedated. You know better than to stroke the downy insides of his arms. You know better than to cover him with the comforter you chose to match his golden eyes. You wait, hoping this sleep takes hold, maybe forever, maybe eternally, for even simple things—leaving your bed, walking out a door—are complicated by a tiger.

This morning at your front door, your tiger pawed for entry. Did you have a choice? Your tiger sounded frightened; your tiger felt endangered. Shhh, you whispered, opening. How about we go downtown?

Put a tiger in a Honda: the car will crash, of course.

Put a tiger in a therapist's office: he roars and runs outside.

Put a tiger on the sidewalk between a Honda and therapist's office: he will try to rip a parking meter from the pavement so he can smash a windshield.

What did you expect? the therapist asked. You married him. Your flesh is thin; you're full of blood. Fangs are always fangs.

Your tiger paced the cobblestones. People pushed strollers across the street.

From the doorstep, the therapist said, Lady, you have two choices:
    Come inside and phone police.
    Or collect your tiger and go.

This was your tiger, for better, for worse. How could you build his cage? Two summers would pass—court orders, new apartments, a parade of brave assistants—before you called police.

Today, you coaxed your tiger through the car door. As you clicked his seatbelt, he sniffed the fine hairs on your neck. You knew the power of your scent. The drive was long. Your tiger growled incessantly, his every "you" sounding like "slut." Forgiveness cut inside your throat, healed, cut again. You knew:
    A tiger's tongue is made of needles.
    A tiger's teeth are blades.
    A tiger injected with Diazepam will eventually fall quiet.

Someday, perhaps, you will be tigerless. Someday, time might fade your tiger's stripes, tame this story to a fable. Someday your friends will return to you, bringing homemade soups. They will study your opposable thumbs, your small, curved jaw, and ask a human question:
    How did a lady like you end up with that tiger?

As if love is a choice of doors: the lady or the tiger. As if you couldn't open both. As if opening and closing doors solved anything at all.

Doors can only change your life onscreen, in game shows, slasher movies. What does a tiger know of doors? This tiger slipped into your house inside upholstered chairs. One moment, you skipped the needle on a favorite album; the floral pattern parted. Instinct made you flinch. Where there was once a Sunday morning, there was now a tiger. A tiger in your living room. A tiger poised to strike. Any sensible lady would have run straight out the door. You did.

The rural roads were sleeting dark. You knew it could be worse. You were frightened. You felt endangered. I'm so sorry, your tiger wept. Can you please come home?

The house you built together was far away, bright with frantic light.

Home again, here you are, unflinching now, unmoving. Your tiger's eyes are closed. Even drugged, he reaches over, pins you to this shredded landscape:

A rumpled bed.

A dirty floor.

An always, always open door.

A door is not a choice. In any story with a tiger, the only certainty is damage. All your human heart can do is fill, empty, fill, beating out the puny kicks of something almost beaten. You know better. It could be worse. Your whole world rests inside this tiger's paw—his claws, for now, retracted.

Red Paint

Toledo, 1984

Someone said he'd drunk ten shots. Someone whispered it only took one. Someone said his mom was redoing the bathroom. Someone said I hope she likes red paint. Someone saw him before it happened, at the choir concert. Someone, a freshman, stood behind him on the risers, the back of his head right there for the touching. Someone forgot the lyrics of the song, staring at the hair curling over his collar. Someone heard that the last song he sang was a Christmas carol, "Still, Still, Still." Someone said and now he is. Someone heard he'd used a fake ID at the hockey rink bar. Someone saw his girlfriend there. Someone said she got in Early Decision, Pre-Med, in California. Someone heard he was waiting on hockey scholarships. Someone heard his girlfriend had blown that goalie from South High. Someone could see it, that's what all her sisters did, those blonde do-gooder sluts. Someone said his girlfriend screamed at him in the parking lot. Someone heard he stood there, heartbroken, and he was crying, like really, really crying. Someone asked, crying? Someone wondered how a girl could shatter the heart of a star goalie and baritone soloist with curly hair that smelled like apples. Someone wanted that kind of power. Someone wished they could still dry his tears. Someone said he flipped her off and got into Mike's car. Someone said they hated Mike. Someone remembered when Mike punched the autistic kid in the lunchroom. Someone wondered how anyone so sweet could be friends with dickhead Mike. Someone said when they got to his house he ran straight to the bathroom. Someone said oh, so he planned it. Someone said no way, never, not a guy like him. Someone heard that his family was off at their cottage. Someone said the gun was in a special locked cabinet. Someone said their dad has one like that. Someone wondered how he broke the lock. Someone said that Mike freaked and ran in and called through the halls until he heard the bathroom door slam. Someone said they knew someone who went to a party there Friday and tripped over paint cans in that hall. Someone joked it was a good thing there were tarps. Would someone please stop making fun? Would someone just shut up? Someone said Mike begged him to open the door. Someone enjoyed picturing dickhead Mike on his knees. Someone said Mike threw the paint cans at the door, trying smash it open. Someone said that must have been so loud. Someone said not as loud as the next sound. Someone said he put the gun in his mouth. Someone said he put it to his temple. Someone said whatever, it worked. Someone wanted to stop talking about it. Why would someone do that? How could someone feel so broken? Someone knew. Someone could hear the silence of the house, the minute after, the morning after—every day was after, now. Someone would have to open that door. Someone would forever be trying.

Hospice

Columbus, 1974

In the room next to mine is a woman in a crib. She is thirty-five years old. She is my aunt. She has never walked nor talked in sentences. Her name is Tawny. I only see her when I visit my grandma, which is a few times a year, and I only see her through the slats of her crib, where she lies on her back, smiling, although sometimes before they close the door, I hear a moan like crying.

I'm happy to be kept out. At Grandma's, I spend nights with my cousin playing Beat the Shark on the blue-white-ocean carpet between couches and eating M&Ms with milk. My cousin and I take baths with pearlescent beads that break open in the water and cap our toes with gummy shells. We set our grandma's electric organ to something called Bossa Nova. We obey Grandma's orders not to open doors—although once, my cousin opens a door and finds our grandpa's shotgun behind it and threatens to shoot me if I move. My younger cousin is a tiny girl with dolly ringlets and no discernable soul. I don't move. Years later, on a bulletin board collaged with grinning friends and puppy pictures, I'll stab out her eyes with a thumbtack.

In the room next to mine, above the woman in the crib, are shelves of Harlequin romances. Rows of pink covers with cursive titles and men nuzzling women's naked necks as if whispering something only skin understands. There must be a thousand thumb-worn spines. Did my grandma sit for hours at Tawny's bedside, wishing to be swept away? I cannot say. To avoid the books is to look at Tawny. To avoid Tawny is to look at the books. I stare at Grandma's blue-white-ocean carpet and sink to quiet depths.

Ask me now about Grandma's house and I'll recall the ocean-carpet, candy, bossa nova, cousin, shotgun, books. I won't mention the adult woman in a crib—a person who was someone's daughter, sister—and I guess, aunt—for a lifetime. In my mind, I can't quite see her. You'd think this image would arrive first. An adult in a crib is notable.

"She got her period you know. That's something your Grandma had to deal with."

That's my mother, always reminding me of people's periods.

But my mother's point is this: a parent's loyalty is a gift the way the sun is a gift—constant and consoling. Last week, I opened a closet at my father's house. Inside were all the books I'd ever given him, forty years' worth, alphabetically arranged and rated, grades noted in pencil. My mother keeps a file cabinet full of all the words I've written, each scrawled story and Christmas list. At any moment she'll cite a poem I penned in 1980. In separate cupboards in separate houses, my parents keep books made by my brother. Books about robots, airships, adventures of a four-year-old girl sketched with braids like mine.

When my parents open doors like these, where am I supposed to look? A parent's loyalty is a gift like the sun is a gift: blinding, near-obliterating.

In 1974, I'm at my Grandma's because in a room across Ohio, there's a boy looking through the slats of his bed. He is my brother. He is thirteen years old. The pain that began in his hip in Little League has metastasized into leukemia. He has gone into remission twice, long enough for us to take a plane across the country and wear sunhats to Disneyland and pose in the shadows of monsters. The year I decide to start forgetting things, I am four and at my Grandma's house while my brother is dying—I'm still learning how to say this—while my brother dies in a hospital bed hours away.

Now, in the room next to mine, my daughters cut snowflakes as I tell you the story of their uncle. I am forty-nine years old. I have never said a word about him. But I'm trying—I'm hoping—I want to tell them his name someday. My kids are a gift the way the sun is a gift: a force that pulls us all together, a terror I'd die without.

At times, it is impossible to look directly at them.

At times, my eyes burn as I sit at my children's bedsides, reading book after book about rescue.

Vigil

Hillcrest Elementary, 2011

The man in the green jacket holds the door. Children with bulky backpacks rush inside, speedy and awkward as baby turtles. Siblings amble in clusters; bigger boys hold lacrosse sticks. Any other morning, the school's front door is a stopper. It's designed to be. It requires a buzz in. It's heavy. It strains their thin arms.

It appears that the man in the green jacket is doing everyone a favor.

"It's nothing," the man in the green jacket says, smiling. Is he a parent? You've never seen him before. He holds the door, smiling, for a very long time.

You keep watching. The man in the green jacket isn't the only one bound by duty.

Everyone thanks the man in the green jacket. Minutes ago, you thanked him, too. Approaching the door, you caught his eye, and he nodded, gentleman-like (for what else is a man holding a door for schoolchildren?). You and your daughter laced fingers and walked in. These days, she finds a classmate and heads off, never turning back. She's in kindergarten. Her classroom is at the other end of the school, through halls crowded with fifth graders who are taller than you. Your daughter is six. She walks the hallway's center line. The crowd closes behind her like a curtain, but still, you wave.

The man in the green jacket holds the door as you exit. He

holds the door as the stragglers arrive. A girl stomps past him, wet-haired, crying. At the curb, the PTO president's van doors sleekly slide as her children unload dioramas. A hatchback stops long enough for the doors to creak open; the driver's head drops as he pulls away, texting.

The man in the green jacket is invisible to everyone but you. Why is he still here? Wouldn't a parent have somewhere to go?

Now, the man holds the door for the flag-raisers, a boy and a girl fumbling with a ladder. No child does this with skill. Once, you watched two boys puzzle over the ropes until one fetched the new principal, a woman with a sharp haircut you've studied more than her name.

The man in the green jacket crosses a line of propriety that isn't easy to explain. (What would you report, exactly? *Excuse me, but that man in the green jacket is being too polite!*) You can't even describe him adequately. "Green jacket" is overbroad. Green as the leaves on the late-budding trees? Green like innocence? Don't dwell on likes. The jacket is army green but not army style. The jacket hangs open over a white t-shirt, khaki pants. The jacket is loose enough to hide things. You could tell a sketch artist about his casual stance, as if he had all the time in the world.

Instead, imagine your daughter has arrived at her classroom (with its large locking closet, its proximity to exits). She's studying the science project: an incubator of chicken eggs. Daily, she describes the chicks' forming lungs, the nourishment of yolk. She finds comfort in measurable facts. Lately, she's gone from sunny and unfazed to perpetually fazed, overwhelmed by social nuances. She's a water balloon in a room full of pins: thin-skinned, swelled with justice. Last year, in Pre-K, adults fixed everything, but in kindergarten, adults do not. She says she's the only one who follows rules. Her seatmates squish her on the bus. Her friends grab her hat during recess. Girls link up in chains that close without her. No matter how many times she's painted into someone else's picture, or saved a seat at lunch, she weeps to you nightly over broken pinkie-promises.

She assumes saviors. She assumes goodness. She does not assume a stranger at a school door is why she practices hiding under desks, silent, as the teacher turns off lights.

Look now. The man in the green jacket has vanished. The door is closed. Is he inside, walking to his child's class—or slipping into a bathroom? Is he loading a grudge—or fiddling with his camera? Has he left the building for work—or for the woods that line the playground?

Best to stay here. You have the time. Soon, you'll have to pull away.

In her classroom, your daughter stands at the incubator, waiting for a peep. Any day now, it will happen: beaks will punch through shells.

It's called an egg-tooth, your daughter corrects, explaining how the heart grows.

Not all of them will hatch, you tell her.

Wait and see, she says.

You do.

Descending

The House of Special Designation, Ekaterinburg, 1918

1.

At night, it's like my head is made of footsteps. Loud and close, then quiet and far, then loud and close again. Like someone climbing stairs. I think of how my sister galloped the stairs of our first house. *Prancing* my grandmother called it, *galloping* my mother called it, *thinking* my sister called it. *I do this so I can think*, she'd say.

Annoying is what I called it. My sister galloped for our whole childhood. Every room on every floor was a pivot in her path, and when our next house had no stairs, she galloped room to room, and when our next house after that had us nearly heaped atop each other, she galloped to every piece of furniture, touched it, galloped on. Near the end, all she could do was walk a circle.

You think a lot for someone who has no ideas, I'd say.

My sister kept moving.

But don't be fooled—my sister had a voice. She sang at the window in the winding staircase in our first house. She screamed when I strung a thread across her path and sliced her ankles.

No one tried to stop her steps. They all just read their books or counted coins or stirred stews or stacked blocks while my sister pranced. It fell to me, alone. So I raised up splinters from the

floorboards. I laid thickets: brother's mudpies, his bloody bandages,
father's family swords.

My sister grew. Her steps got louder, heavier, like wet snow fall-
ing in clumps from trees to the rooftop—or what, under your thin
blankets, shuddering in your thin bed, you hope to be wet snow.

I grew, too. I stretched to fill our shrinking rooms as best I could.

2.

Hardest to bear is the view from our windows.

We used to stroll among fountains. Grandmother's roses dizzied
the bees. Every room spilled with blooms sent by toadying bota-
nists. After that, they let us rake a garden. We planted beets. How
funny it is to mourn the feel of soil warmed by sunlight. I miss the
bend of stems.

Today, our view is a wooden fence. Plank after plank of palisade,
dull as the beef we're given. We're pinned to the edges of routine. It
sounds strange, but I admire the way our youngest sister loops as
she likes. At least her path is hers.

The only softness in the days is ours—our dimples, our curls,
our simple dresses. We're allowed to sew, and so we circle together
as our brother, at our ankles, sails ships.

Come here, butterfly, Mother says to our youngest sister. *Light
upon this sofa, sit a while. Let's mend.*

We pull seams, mark hems, gather ruffles. My favorite gown is
blue, like parrot feathers. I haven't worn it since the War. I rip out
the neck.

Shall I tell you the secret of our dresses?

See my hands?

Look. With every stitch, we drop a diamond. We plant heir-
looms beneath our pleats and tuck our waists with topaz.

When a guard looks in, we rest our hands and raise our eyebrows. We daughters have a wager. Which of us will be the first to draw a smile from those beards? Who will catch and hold a gaze?

Outside, the guards stand in rows. Inside, we stab sleeves with pins.

It would only take a swaying skirt to pull a guard out of line. To remind us all of curves, of softness. To poke a hole. An opening.

3.

What I saw today made me drop the eggs.

Yes, the girls, now women, have done worse. Cooking for them, I know things. It's not my place to gossip. I cannot say which or what or who. But last summer, a middle daughter refused my bread, just like my wife did until things took hold. My wife's sickness ended with our fat twins. The middle daughter's sickness just ended. Done. Right after Doctor visited.

The things I know.

But today. Today spilled us over.

How to tell it?

I'll say this. A guard left a box in a hole by the palisade. This guard stood watch. Then the youngest daughter, the one who skips, skipped along. The family's morning walk. The third time round, she ran ahead. She stopped. Looked about. Stooped and opened the little box.

And then she smiled.

Smiled at the guard!

These pigs with guns trained on our heads!

Look at that bell tower! See the muzzle? They're on every roof-top. The drunkest guard, there, fondles his bayonet.

It's a chore just carrying eggs to the stove!

Next thing, the daughter pulled out something small and white and round. Popped it in her mouth. Ate another.

Teacakes. Nine or ten from the looks of it.

I about fell through the shutters.

All they let me do is boil. What I'd give to build a torte! Any food from the nuns, the guards gobble and belch like cannon fire. These pigs rut with women steps away from our bedrooms.

But not this guard.

Not this daughter.

This guard smiled and tipped his cap.

This daughter skipped away laughing.

Yes, I dropped the eggs. Yes, I lost all but three.

Everything here could break open at any minute.

Please, I beg you, save us from this mess.

4.

I dreamt the bars on the windows turned into piano keys. I played them. I banged my hands and music rang. *No, Son!* Mother cried. *You will bruise! Son, stop this very instant!* Father laughed, *My son, how do you know that song?* I played Concerto No. 2. I beat the bars to clanging. My fingers purpled. They swelled like sausages. I played on. My sisters came after me with blankets, stacks of blankets, stacks so high they blocked my sisters' faces. My sisters swaddled me as if I were on fire. I ran. I flew through the doors, beyond the fence, out into the driveway. The blankets fell away. I felt the breeze on my face. Our dogs gave chase. The music became the guards' drunk singing *Their thrones are covered with blood!* My fingers swelled until they split and Mother screamed, *Put the blood back inside my son or he is going to die!* Pebbles spat from the ground at my feet. I ran faster than the gunshots.

5.

No, he did not look like a man out for blood. He was a modest man. He had kind eyes. His beard was threaded black and white, but overgrown—I thought at first he was a servant.

He had to carry the sickly son out to the garden, but the son was too old for carrying. In those moments he was neither tsar nor murderer—just a father stooped beneath a weight no father should bear. He had to place the boy precisely to prevent a bruise. Once, I stepped from my post to help.

This set the Commandant yapping. *Put these idle rich to work! They thirst for our blood!*

Yet in truth their thirst was simple.

All you had to do was meet their eyes and they would smile. It was like they thanked you just for seeing them. For looking past their gold chains our Commandant picked and pocketed.

All they wanted was someone to talk with.

So I did.

I used to carry my aunt uphill to market, I told him. *She lived on air and yet each time I swore she'd ate a fatted pig.*

He laughed and I could tell that, were we elsewhere, he'd have shook my hand.

The next day as she rounded the path, I asked the skipping daughter what she'd name her dog's new puppies.

She flew past. But the next time around, she whispered:

Honey, Pudding, Cake, Cake the Second, Cake the Third.

This I understood.

The skipping daughter had freckles you couldn't see unless you got close. Each day, near me, she slowed a little more. I could see her boots had mended holes. Inside my own worn boots, my toes curled. I prayed I wouldn't have to break her wings.

6.

Pull the laces: 1-2-3-4-5-6-7 plus 8-9-10-11 and now another pull for 12.

Pull again to lock in luck: mother-father-brother-sister-sister-sister-me plus cook-doctor-maid-footman and one more for—.

For 12.

For him.

(He gave me fine new boots!)

You've worn your boots to shreds by skipping, Miss A, he said. *Your wings need feathering.*

(He sees my wings!)

Well, of course he does. A good Guard understands his fellow Guardian.

But he is the only one who does. Mother, father can't be bothered. Sister spies and tries to clip me. Trips, slips, my brother's ships: wrecks I weave my rudder through.

My duty is undying.

My steps are our safekeeping.

I trench the tracks of fortune's wheel.

He stands his post by the fence. I pace my post indoors.

My rounds:

> 60 steps for sisters' safety.
>
> Father: 50.
>
> Bruising brother, miserable mother: 700 steps apiece.
>
> Cook and maid: 30 table taps.
>
> Doctor, footman: 40 more.
>
> For myself: 17 for all my years, plus one more—a prayer for better birthdays.

(He brought me teacakes for my birthday!)

With every breach, I start over: when the drunk guard knocked off Father's cap. When Father stooped to get it. When the fat guard sings about our death. When Mother's maid weeps. When Mother rages. When they fire guns to wake our puppies. When they shoot my windowsill.

I start over.

I am Tyche, winged, powerful. I alone can steer our fate.

See how well I've done? My steps secured our secret savior.

He calls me *Miss A.*

He gave me teacakes.

(He says he will set us free!)

He brought me boots to lace so I can pace. Good boots make a good Guardian.

For our protection, I pull the laces: 1-2-3-4-5-6-7 plus 8-9-10-11. And now another pull for 12.

7.

When my children reach for me, I become something different. Something whole, engulfing. For lack of more artful expression, I become my heart. Or perhaps I mean that my children become my heart.

This month was so trying, decorum crashed against the white-washed windowpanes and splintered into screams. *All we want is air,* I'd plead. *Just a crack of the window, please?* Me, the Empress, reduced to begging a factory oaf who bragged of the gun in his trousers. *But where is it, Sir? Your gun must be tiny,* my Tatiana asked. Impertinent girl. If we die, we will go laughing.

My children wear brave faces and now I fear they'll never know how proud I am.

How we've shrunk to fit inside this emptiness. Even Alexei stopped tempting fate with his leaps, feigning pleasure in a succession of chairs. Olga's tempers folded, square by square, into sharp corners. Maria, as ever, ministered to our needs, her hands constant, open, steady.

Busy Nastia charmed the guards by herding us. One young guard brought her new boots. What was I to do? The lines of propriety shift like shadows.

Last night, he and his cohort were dismissed, replaced with foreigners. These new guards are blank as iron skillets—they do not charm.

At midnight, they brought us to this basement.

What happens next?

You might think our hearts are hard as the diamonds sewn into our dresses. You would be wrong. Diamonds do not create darkness—diamonds can only reflect.

Now, the Commandant reads a statement.

Now, my husband asks me, *What?*

Now, the room explodes.

Now, when my children reach for me, we bleed like watercolors. We are footfalls in wet soil—last words trapped inside a mother's heart.

On and on we pulse.

We soak.

We fade.

Swath

I. Supercell

The tornado craved fame. Snug in its supercell, drinking in warmth, the young cyclone could practically taste the kitten it would pluck from a windowsill and cradle in branches, its white fur pristine save for a lick of mud on its nose—the tornado's signature—all of this, mind you, while toothpicking barns and milkshaking cows and scrambling countless coops. The tornado would explode shoe closets, festoon fences. It would pop ears of corn on the stalk.

Its swath would be one of charming collisions. The paparazzi would dodge peony petals and pose by a tower of playground slides. The tornado would be known as *An F4 With Finesse!*

Of course, the dreams of cyclones are as changeable as, well, the wind. But please understand: the tornado did not seek mayhem. Other tornadoes wanted the worst kind of attention. They stabbed, they pulverized, they orphaned. They aimed for zoos and hospitals, stadiums and traffic jams. You could hear it in their brutish roar: OBLITERATE.

Not you, tsked the supercell. *Your greatness does not arise from the suffering of others.*

Also, the tornado did not seek justice. Some tornadoes spun statements: The stones unearthed for your black-bottom pool? Requarried. Your windows? Sand. What you disturb, I shall restore.

The swaths of those self-righteous storms bloomed with sunflowers and kale.

Nobody likes a scold, said the supercell, hailing stones the size of baby heads. A lucky guess, since the supercell could not measure an actual baby's head.

Now the supercell spat icy downdrafts. It inhaled steam from drenched summer roads. *Go,* it thundered to the cyclone. *Show them what you're made of.*

II. Stretch

The tornado dipped into low green skies. It touched the ground. The earth was sharp, surprisingly so—for what can a cyclone know of edges? The tornado curled into a question mark, like the mystery of tornadogenesis itself: Will you dissolve into wisps, withdraw? Will you rage?

Time was short. The supercell plumped it with lightning, rain, and the tornado dropped to the tree line. The tornado stretched its throat. It tasted breakage. It tasted a hundred years of sunlight, the scars made by lesser storms, lightning char. It tasted the dark death of heartwood, the snap of saplings, roots and soil, fur-lined burrows. It swallowed the emptiness of sockets.

Who can predict how a tornado—young and full of itself—will funnel its velocity? Not the chasers with their cameras. Not the dots of Doppler. Not even the supercell who gives the tornado life. Who feeds it, and is fed.

And so, the tornado feasted on the holes it made. It wanted to make more.

III. Twist

The speed. The swirl. The spread. The sound. Everywhere its roar, its width, its pull, its push, its force. All the tornado was supposed to do or be simply was. It was everything and the absence of everything. As it consumed, it learned: the yearning in rooftops shingled by men too young to grow good beards. The weariness soaked into bathtubs. The outrage bolted into door locks. The terror squeezed into teddy bears. The anxiety paced into threadbare rugs and poured into flasks wedged behind textbooks. In one gulp, the tornado swallowed all the flirtation and humiliation of the city pool. The shame of locker rooms. The sweat of bean fields. The despair chalked into concrete courts in the prison rec yard.

Yes, the tornado could do better than kittens. It could absorb anguish, remove what those on earth believed already ruined. Benevolence pulsed its vortex. The paparazzi would be most grateful of all: *Tornado Damage—or Woe: Be Gone?*

It headed northeast, towards the airport, the endless echoes of *Goodbye* and *Please Come Back.*

Suddenly, the tornado pulled south. The paparazzi reversed, cameras jittering. The tornado was two miles wide.

Nearby was a wellspring of deep, maybe endless, grief. The tornado veered towards the place. There were rows of stones etched with names, names, names, some faded, some freshly crisp. The new-mown grass was planted with flags and plastic flowers. Below the lawn, the loam itself was layered with centuries of torment. The tornado was drawn by the pain of leaving—and the anticipation of such pain.

Keep in mind: a tornado swallowing human sorrow would grow beyond all measure. How would it ever stop? It wouldn't—unless something intervened.

Everything in this world must end, soothed the supercell, wrapping its cold arms tight. The tornado choked. Stunned, it roped above the headstones, thinning, breaking up. Nothing more than unripe apples fell into its wake.

IV. Swath

The sirens stopped and neighbors blinked in shafts of blinding sunlight. They stepped through broken panes of glass to find children, mothers, brothers, stepdads, teachers. They held onto one another's rain-soaked shirts with everything they had. The paparazzi marveled: not a single road blocked, nobody injured, yet cars crumpled and buildings collapsed. The evening news zoomed in on a bird's nest balanced atop a flamingo floatie, every egg intact. In the end, the tornado was certainly *A Fastidious F4!*

Now, people hugged their pets and cleared debris, but no one talked about the storm. The thing they'd felt was just too strange to mention. How would they even phrase it? How did a person use language, that rude music, to describe the sheer elation when the funnel passed, that laughter in the marrow, that relief of pent-upness, the wash of—it's impossible, isn't it, when you're huddled in your basement and the roof of your house unzips, to feel, well, something just like—pleasure?

No one knew what to say, so no one did. But the tornado made its mark. A child felt it as she walked outside, stepping in her father's footsteps, holding her mother's hand. She spotted brightness in the wreckage: a propeller blade bent into a smile, gleaming right at her.

What a mess, her parents sighed.

If the girl had the power to name the world, she'd have called it something different. She sat with her parents, sifting. They unearthed strangers' photos, sorted them by hairstyle. They gathered, paired, mourned, returned. Every so often, they watched the sky for the quiet pink parting of clouds.

Acknowledgements

Works in this collection have appeared, with slight variations, in the following anthologies and journals:

7x7: "Descending: The House of Special Designation, Ekaterinburg, 1918" (as "Descending," an exquisite-corpse game in collaboration with visual artist Maeve D'Arcy)

Carve: "Vigil: Hillcrest Elementary, 2011" (Under the title "Vigil")

Fiction Southeast: "Dreamland: Coney Island, 1904"

Gigantic Sequins: "Feather Rousing"

Hobart (rpt. in *HAD): "*Hospice: Columbus, 1974"

Hobart (rpt. in *HAD):* "Swath"

Hope is the Thing: Wisconsinites on Perseverance in a Pandemic, edited by B.J. Hollars, Wisconsin Historical Society Press, Fall 2021: "Plumage: Green Bay, 2020" (Under the title "Hope is the Hawaiian Shirt, Hope is the Ukulele")

Sundog Lit: "Red Paint: Toledo, 1984" (Under the title "Red Paint")

Superstition Review: "The Lady, The Tiger: Cincinnati, 1999" (Under the title "The Lady, The Tiger")

A small number of these pieces appeared in the limited-edition chapbook *Morbid Curiosities*, 2014, *New Delta Review* press (out-of-print).

Quotes regarding the life of Charles Valentin Alkan can be traced to multiple sources, including the blog post, "The Myths of Alkan, Transcript of a Talk for BBC Radio 3" by Jack Gibbons (2002), and *Charles Valentin Alkan: His Life and His Music*, by William Alexander Eddie (United Kingdom, Taylor & Francis, 2017).

Author's Note of Gratitude
The author is deeply grateful to the editors who first published these pieces in journals, and to Diane Goettel at Black Lawerence Press for giving this hybridiary a home. She's especially delighted to thank her editor, Lisa Fay Coutley, for her guidance and general ferocity.

She thanks Ruth, David, Chuck, Gwendolyn, and Madelyn—along with her family, friends, and colleagues—for their love, support, and general ferocity as well.

Kara Counard

REBECCA MEACHAM's short story collection, *Let's Do*, won UNT Press's Katherine Anne Porter Prize in Fiction, and her flash fiction collection, *Morbid Curiosities*, won the *New Delta Review* chapbook prize. Her work has appeared most recently in *Best Microfiction 2021*, *Wigleaf*, *HAD*, and *Gigantic Sequins*, and her prose has been set to music, translated into Polish, and carved into woodblocks and letter-pressed by steamroller. She is a professor of English at the University of Wisconsin-Green Bay, where she directs The Teaching Press and chairs the B.F.A. in Writing and Applied Arts program.